The Rebound Chick

Seante Evans

Dedication

This book is dedicated to my late Nana, Jackie Howard. You were the glue to this family, and I miss you so much. Your wisdom and guidance allowed me to be the strong, independent woman I am today. I love you. Watch over my mother up there, keep looking down on us, and shining your light through your spirit.

PS: Can you find a better pop-up spot in my house because you have been loving my wall by the steps? My ladybug in heaven.

Contents

Introduction: A Temporary High 1

Chapter 1 Malik 2

Chapter 2 Jeremiah 15

Chapter 3 Elijah 23

Chapter 4 Caleb 28

Chapter 5 Aaron 32

Chapter 6 Carter 36

Chapter 7 Boy Bye 41

Introduction

A Temporary High

When it comes to dating, Tiffany can tell you firsthand that it's no walk in the park. That first meet and greet can feel like the best thing in the world—asking questions like, "What's your favorite color?" or "What do you like and don't like?" This is typically how dating plays out. But for Tiffany, she's starting to realize that dates and conversations are really just that—dates and conversations.

Most of the time, women are known to be the side piece, but in this case, we're now called the rebound chick. The black version of a rebound chick means when a guy tries to wine and dine you, but really has his eyes on someone else. You're just helping him get over his last heartbreak until he can be with who he really wants to be with. You're just an in the meantime..in between time; until he's ready to move along.

Tiffany knows what she brings to the table. She was taught never to let a man walk over you or use you. Too late, though—because if being used had a face, Tiffany would have that award. So, with that being said, "You ready? Here we go." Let's see how Tiffany holds the title of a true rebound chick.

CHAPTER 1

Malik

A long time ago, Tiffany made a vision board. On that board, she mapped out her whole life—house, car, baby, job, husband, good income. She knew that one day, she'd make that vision come true. But it seemed like every year, something would be added or taken off her vision board. At one point, she felt like she just couldn't get it right, no matter how many times she changed it. Even talking to her friends, she was starting to feel like there would never be someone who could check everything off her list.

One night, Tiffany's friend Rachel invited her over for a party. This was Rachel's annual list party, where the girls would sit around, eat, and talk about what they were looking for in a man. Sometimes they'd even paint their ideal man on a canvas. There was only one man who fit Tiffany's description, and that was Morris Chestnut. If she found him, she knew she'd be just fine. Lord knows she had watched *The Best Man* a million times. Tiffany was detailed: a good job, a good car, a passport, a house, sexy, well-dressed, and treats her with respect. Rachel took a look at Tiffany's list and told her she was missing a lot of important details when it came to finding a good man. Now, granted, Rachel was single, but she'd had her share of bad relationships and knew she had to school Tiffany on creating the perfect list.

After tweaking her list and adding some key details, Tiffany was ready to sit back and see what happened next. After a long day of work, Tiffany and her girls decided to go to a fair to enjoy some good food and have a fun night out. While enjoying the food and rides, Tiffany noticed a man looking at her. Rachel asked, "You see what I see?" Tiffany replied, "I see, but I'm not going over there." While walking to the bathroom, Tiffany and the guy bumped into each other. "Ah, excuse you, watch where you're going." "I'm sorry," he replied.

As Tiffany walked back to her friends, the guy called out, "My name's Malik." Even though she acted like she was ignoring him, she definitely heard him. Rachel looked at Tiffany, trying to figure out what had happened in the bathroom. While riding more rides, Tiffany saw Malik staring at her again. Her friends were all like, "I saw that," "Saw what?" Tiffany asked. "We see that man looking at you." Tiffany said, "Girl, he's nobody, just some guy I bumped into in the bathroom." After the fair, Tiffany didn't think too much about Malik, especially since she didn't even tell him her name. The next day, what would have been a typical Monday turned into a meet-and-greet, or should I say, a bump-into-greet. While shopping at Walmart, Tiffany couldn't help but notice someone looking at her.

Not thinking too much about it, she approached the guy and asked, "Can I help you?" He quickly replied, "You don't remember me, do you?" "Should I?" she asked. "I'm Malik; we met at the fair last week." "Oh, nice to see you again." As they just stared at each other, Malik slowly asked, "What's your name?" Tiffany cleared her throat and said, "My name is Tiffany." She then asked him if there was something she could help him with. Malik looked at her and said, "I would love to take you out for dinner." Just to hurry up and get him out of her face, she gave him her number and told him he could call her. As he walked away, Tiffany thought to herself, "Damn, I should've given him a fake name and number." She just knew he wasn't going to use the number, let alone ask to take her out on a date.

A few days later, Tiffany received a text from Malik asking if she was free for dinner. She responded, "Yes, I'm free. You can pick me up at 7 pm. What do you have a taste for?" He replied, "I wouldn't mind getting some baby back ribs." When Tiffany looked back at her text, she realized she told him he could pick her up. She thought for a moment and said to herself, "Nope. This isn't going to happen." She quickly called him and said, "Hey, I'll meet you at the restaurant."

They decided to keep it simple and went to Chili's for something to eat. Tiffany arrived 10 minutes late, just because. When she saw him, she approached him with a firm hug and asked how he had been doing. As they went inside to sit down, Tiffany was already thinking she was ready to go home. However, she told herself she was going to make the best of it. At this point, she had given up on men and felt like they were all the same. But she was willing to put all that behind her and take a chance on someone new.

Dinner went better than either of them expected, and after the bill came, Malik was already asking to see Tiffany again. Just like that, they were setting up for date number two. She knew she wanted to keep things to herself because she had no idea how things were going to go between the two of them. After about two months of casual dating, Malik was ready to take things to the next level and become a couple.

At night, when the apartment got too quiet, Tiffany would pull out her list and read it like a prayer. Some nights it felt like armor; other nights it felt like a mirror, showing her the places she still needed to heal. She wanted the man she wrote down—steady, respectful, grown—but the silence had its own opinion. It told her to settle. It told her to text somebody who didn't deserve another chance. She'd breathe, put the phone face down, and circle the same word again: respect.

The list wasn't just bullet points; it was a promise she made to herself in the middle of lonely Fridays and slow Sundays. She wrote consistency over chemistry and underlined peace over potential headaches. Then she'd check the door locks, turn off the TV, and remind herself that waiting well is still movement—that choosing loneliness for a season was better than living lonely with the wrong person. She already had a lifetime filled with regret.

This time, she would choose herself before she chose a situation. She would move slow, listen for consistency, and honor her list. She would open her heart with boundaries, not walls. And when love showed up, it would meet her where she stood—whole, steady, and ready.

Tiffany wasn't 100% sure if that was what she was ready for, so she chose to wait another two weeks before they became official. When she finally told her friends, they told her they already knew and were happy for her.

Within six months of being a couple, Malik put the offer on the table for them to move in together. Tiffany felt like it was way too soon, but even though she still had about three weeks left on her lease and her rent was going up, she agreed and told him, "Fine, let's do it."

After searching, they found a one-bedroom, one-bathroom apartment. They agreed to help each other with the bills and split everything down the middle. Everything was fine in the beginning, until Malik came home one day and said he had lost his job and Tiffany would have to handle the bills.

"I knew something like this was going to happen," Tiffany yelled out. Malik tried to defend himself by telling her it wasn't his fault.

As time went on, Malik still wasn't working, and when he did find a job, it was labor-ready, where they paid out the same day you worked. Tiffany had had enough and wanted to stay with her friends for a while. Little did she know, Malik wasn't going to let her leave that easily. When he saw her packing her bags, he yelled in rage, "You're not leaving me!" Tiffany snapped back, "Nigga, I don't know who the hell you think you're talking to, but you better get your ass out of my face."

"You think you're crazy? I'll show you crazy," she added. Not only was this a side of Tiffany he'd never seen, but it was also a side of Malik she'd never seen either. She never imagined she would be in love with a man who was verbally abusive. That was a chapter in her life she'd never dealt with before, and if he thought for one second she was going to put up with it, it wasn't going to happen. He must have forgotten she'd been taught by the best how to shoot a gun.

When Tiffany finally packed her bag, she left while Malik was asleep and drove to her friend Rachel's house. When Malik woke up and saw that Tiffany was gone, he called her over 20 times and sent text messages. After two days, Tiffany was ready to go back home and work things out with her man. When she got home, Malik was sitting on the couch, drinking a beer and playing the game. As she walked in, she saw that he was looking at her, waiting for an explanation.

"Malik, I know you're mad, but I needed some time to take everything in." Without saying anything back, Tiffany walked to their bedroom and unpacked her bag. Malik finally came into the bedroom, ready to talk. "It's been two days, Tiffany, where have you been?" he shouted, his anger boiling over. "Malik, chill out. I was at Rachel's house," Tiffany replied calmly. The hurt and pain in their eyes made it clear that neither of them knew what to say next. They could only cry and walk away from each other.

After dinner, they both agreed that they wouldn't yell at each other anymore and would work through their problems respectfully. Tiffany's biggest concern was that Malik find a job so all the pressure wouldn't be on her. Little did she know that while she was gone, he had gotten a call about a job. The pay wasn't much, but it was something. It was a third-shift job, which meant Tiffany would be home alone at night. She didn't like it, but she would adjust to it.

Their relationship had become boring, bane, and mundane—work, sleep, eat, and occasionally they would have sex. And even that was about a 4, maybe a 5, depending on how she was feeling. They both knew they had a lot of work to do if they wanted their relationship to work. Tiffany felt like this was the new norm, but she wasn't going to complain or fuss about it because she didn't want to fight.

After about three months of working, unfortunately, the company that Malik was working for closed down. Once again, he was out of a job, and the bills were back on her. Tiffany couldn't handle this again, so instead of going to a friend's house, she felt they should break up. Malik didn't want things to end between them. Deep down, he knew there was a great-paying job out there for him. He also knew he would lose the apartment if Tiffany left because the company had only given them a month's worth of pay.

While driving to Rachel's house, Tiffany kept beating herself up for taking such a big step in their relationship. Moving in together should have been the last thing on her mind. She knew she was deeply in love with Malik. This was the first time she had felt this kind of love. But she also knew when she was feeling used and taken advantage of. Before he treated her like an ATM, she knew it was best to just leave.

A few months had passed since Tiffany left Malik, and she thought about him every day. She wanted to know how he was doing, and most importantly, she wanted to know where he was staying. She wanted to call him a few times, but she knew he wasn't going to answer her call. Then, one day on Facebook, she saw that the job he had been waiting for had finally come through. He had found not only his dream job but a well-paying one. As bad as she wanted to call him, she didn't want him to think she wanted him back for his money. So, instead of calling him, she decided to send him a "Congratulations" message via inbox. He responded quickly, saying, "Thank you." Instead of continuing the conversation on social media, she decided to call him.

As soon as she heard Malik's voice, her heart melted, and she felt nothing but butterflies. He told her that he missed her and wanted to see her, and she felt the same. Even though she had no idea how things were going to play out, she was just excited to see the man that she loved. When she arrived at his new place, she was shocked at how far he had turned his life around. The first thing she wanted him to know was that she didn't come because she wanted him back or wanted his money. Before she could get all of her words out, he embraced her with a soft kiss and started to apologize. He explained that he never wanted her to feel like she had to be the breadwinner. Malik knew Tiffany was the love of his life and that he would do or say anything to get her back.

Tiffany believed everything Malik was saying. She even told him she had never heard him speak this apologetically before. After a long talk, she agreed to get back together, but they would take things slow and make it clear that they would not live together. Tiffany told Malik that it was best for her to keep her place, and she would come and spend the night a few nights a week. Even though Malik wanted her back home with him, he was willing to respect her wishes.

Things were finally back to how they were when they first got together. No fighting, no yelling, no calling each other out of their names. Every day, Tiffany felt like packing her things and moving back in with Malik, but she didn't want to risk something going wrong. The more they spent time together, the closer she felt to him. Could this be the one? She asked herself. There were times when she wanted to ask Malik if he ever thought about marriage. But instead of

Malik

questioning him, she decided to ask her friends what their take on marriage was. Even though none of her friends had ever been married before, they definitely had watched enough movies and TV shows. There were even times when Tiffany would find herself watching Tyler Perry movies like *Why Did I Get Married* and love stories like *The Notebook*. Yes, she grew up around parents and grandparents who had amazing marriages, but in 2024, relationships weren't like that anymore. Most marriages these days only last 4 to 5 years. Couples spend more time in the courthouse than in their own house. So instead of worrying, she just let it run its course.

One night, Malik called Tiffany and told her to get her hair and nails done. Afterward, she was supposed to go out and buy a new dress, and he was going to pay for everything. Tiffany, confused, called her friend Rachel because she had no idea what all this was about. It wasn't her birthday, nor was it their anniversary. Little did she know, Rachel had already known what was going on and had to keep everything a secret. After Tiffany got everything done, Rachel decided to come over and help her get ready for the evening. Tiffany still had no idea what was going on or why Rachel was helping her get ready for a date.

When Malik came to pick Tiffany up, Rachel had already warned her not to ask a bunch of questions and just enjoy the night. Malik had made reservations at a very upscale restaurant called LaRita's. Since they had been dating, they had always talked about eating there but had never actually done it. As they arrived at the restaurant, Tiffany felt nothing but butterflies. Although curious, she still didn't question what was going on. As they began placing their orders, Tiffany was trying to take in all the delicious options on the menu. She ended up ordering salmon, greens, and a loaded baked potato, while Malik ordered a nice steak dinner. After they finished eating, the waiter came over and asked if they would be having dessert. Tiffany, feeling full, said she couldn't eat another bite.

When the waiter walked away, the manager came to the table and asked if they had enjoyed their meal, and hoped they would come back in the future. Before leaving, Tiffany went to use the bathroom, and when she came back, she saw a small box sitting in front of her chair. Malik had already asked the manager if they could play Tiffany's song, "Happily Ever After" by Case. As soon as the song started playing,

Tiffany began crying and said to herself, "This can't be happening." Malik got up, got down on one knee, and asked Tiffany for her hand in marriage. She looked into his eyes and said an ecstatic, "YES!" The entire restaurant started clapping for them as Malik swept her off her feet and carried her to the car. She called all her family and friends to share the good news.

Tiffany was so excited; she wanted to start making plans right away. From finding a location and a dress to picking out her bridesmaids and flower girls, she was ready to dive in. Malik had to calm her down because she was completely overwhelmed. Tiffany had checked off everything on her vision board. Now, granted, Malik wasn't Morris, but she was finally happy. Within five months of their engagement, Tiffany had moved back into the house with Malik. She found her dress and had the whole wedding party picked out. Things were still going well between them until Tiffany asked Malik if they could go on a date, and he said no. She had been working hard for a while and needed to unwind that night.

Malik took Tiffany into the kitchen and showed her on the calendar all the bills he had paid that week. Tiffany said, "So, are you saying I can't have a night to unwind?" Without answering her, Malik just walked away and started playing the video game. Instead of starting a fight, Tiffany ran a hot bubble bath, poured a glass of wine, and played some jazz music. Tears began pouring down her face because she had been under a lot of stress and just wanted to unwind with her fiancé. She was trying to look past the signs of verbal abuse again, but he was just ignoring her.

After her bath, she went to bed and wrote in her journal about how she was feeling. The next morning, while fixing her breakfast, Tiffany was debating whether she should talk to her fiancé about last night. She knew the outcome of speaking up, but didn't want to go to work stressed and worried about home. While she was on break, Malik called to ask her if she could grab dinner to bring home because he was going to be late. Immediately, she fired back, "Why are you going to be late?" He hung up the phone with no response. "Oh, this what we doing? I got something for him."

When Tiffany got off work, she stopped by McDonald's and ordered him a cheeseburger Happy Meal with milk, and she ordered herself a quarter-pounder with cheese. Once she got home and walked into the house, she called Malik's name and told him it was time for dinner. When Malik walked into the kitchen and saw what Tiffany had brought for him to eat, he said, "What is this?" Tiffany responded, "Since you want to act like a child, I'm going to treat you like a child."

"Are you trying to be funny?" Malik was beyond pissed at Tiffany. "Do you have any idea how it feels to work all day and come home to this BS?" Malik had started to turn back into the man that Tiffany didn't want to be around, but she knew she couldn't pack her bags and leave this time.

Deep down inside, Tiffany still knew that Malik was the love of her life and that she wanted to spend the rest of her life with him. She kept asking herself how someone could go from 0-100 that fast. She knew what she was doing when she brought him the happy meal and expected him to react to it, but yelling was not what she was expecting. After finally letting him cool off, she walked to the living room and asked him what he would really like to have for dinner. Malik looked at her and said, "I'll just make a sandwich and get ready for bed."

The next day, Tiffany knew it was time to call a therapist to get them some counseling before they got married. She had heard about this great marriage counselor named Dr. James, and he was the best in town. Even though she didn't talk to Malik, she made the appointment and told him where to meet her. Malik was beyond blindsided about what was going on, but he was willing to sit through the session and let her express how she had been feeling.

When it was Malik's turn to express how he was feeling, he didn't say much. He expressed how she was the love of his life and that he wanted to spend the rest of his life with her. Dr. James gave them an assignment to do before their next session. Their assignment was to take a piece of paper and write their pros and cons about each other and see which one outweighed the other. Getting Malik to do the assignment was going to be like pulling teeth, but she was going to try. They had two days to get it done. And just like that, he did not complete the assignment.

Still trying to save their relationship before getting married was going to take some time. Tiffany knew she didn't want to have a long engagement. After a few more sessions with Dr. James and at-home assignments to complete, Tiffany felt it was best to call off the wedding. She felt that nothing was getting better between them and saw herself fixing things alone. Before going to bed, she prayed harder than she ever had and asked God for a sign. When she woke up the next morning, she saw that Malik had fixed her breakfast and lunch as if he had changed overnight. She thought, "Maybe the prayer really worked!"

She had always believed in the power of prayer. As she asked herself if God had changed her man overnight, only time would tell. When she got home, she had already decided she didn't want to cook dinner. Turns out Malik had beaten her to it. Not only did he fix dinner, but he also ran her a hot bubble bath so she could relax and topped the night off with a massage. She didn't know what was making Malik do all of this, but she was going to enjoy it.

After a few days, Tiffany asked Malik if they could just go get married at the courthouse and have a big wedding later. Without thinking too much into it, he agreed, and before they knew it, they were downtown applying for their marriage license. Tiffany was smiling from ear to ear because she couldn't wait to be Malik's wife. Once their license came in the mail, they made an appointment to go to the courthouse. Even though it was bad timing and most of their friends didn't agree with them going to the courthouse, there was nothing that was going to stop their happiness. With their big day approaching, the only thing that was missing was asking her dad to walk her down the aisle.

"Dad, can you walk me down the aisle?" "No, baby girl, I'm sorry I have to work." She was crushed, but she understood. They knew they didn't want to change the date because it was a special moment for them.

On April 13, 2012, it was finally time to say "I do" and become Mrs. Tiffany Miller. After their courthouse ceremony, they called their family and friends, inviting them to join them for a nice dinner. Seeing all their loved ones together made Tiffany's heart swell—her day was finally perfect.

About seven months into their marriage, Tiffany woke up one morning feeling sick and couldn't figure out why. Thinking it was food poisoning, she quickly made a doctor's appointment. But to her surprise, what she thought was food poisoning turned out to be a baby! Tiffany was already eight weeks pregnant. Though it wasn't the news she had been expecting, she was relieved that she and Malik's finances were in a good place. Excited, she called Malik as soon as she got in the car to share the news. When she got home, they both started calling friends and family to spread their joy.

In the middle of making calls, Tiffany suddenly felt a sharp pain in her stomach. When she stood up, she saw blood. Panic set in as she screamed, "Malik! I'm bleeding! Call 911!" Stunned, Malik quickly dialed for an ambulance. Once they arrived at the hospital, the doctor reassured them that everything was fine—the bleeding was just her body finishing out a final period.

From that moment on, Tiffany's prayer was simple: to have a safe and healthy pregnancy. At seven months, everything seemed to be going smoothly until she started experiencing Braxton Hicks contractions. As a precaution, her doctor placed her on bed rest for the remainder of the pregnancy.

One night, 1:00 am to be exact, intense contractions woke Tiffany up. She called the doctor, who advised her not to come in unless her contractions were 3 to 5 minutes apart. But Tiffany didn't care what the doctor said—she told Malik, "I want to go now." The hospital was 15 minutes away, but Malik drove like it was just around the corner.

Even though her water hadn't broken, Tiffany knew this pain was unlike anything she had ever felt before. As soon as they arrived, the hospital staff rushed her to labor and delivery. After about three hours, the doctor decided it was time to break her water. The contractions hit faster and harder, and she was dilating quickly.

After twelve hours of grueling labor, Tiffany gave birth to a healthy baby boy, Jaxon Pierce Miller, weighing 7 lbs. 5 oz. Tears of joy were all she felt that entire day, and she couldn't wait to take him home. Tiffany looked forward to bonding with her son, even though everyone was already saying he looked like Malik.

Being a father was a feeling Malik had always longed for. Every time he went to the store, he came home with a new toy or outfit—he was definitely going to win Daddy of the Year for sure. Once they were discharged from the hospital and arrived home, Tiffany finally took in the reality—she had gone from a wife to a mother within their first year of marriage.

Malik

When Malik went back to work, Tiffany was home alone with baby Jaxon. Between bottle-feeding and diaper changes, motherhood quickly became overwhelming. She had no idea she was experiencing postpartum depression. She called her mother and mother-in-law, desperate for help during the day. She was always told, "When the baby sleeps, you sleep." But instead of resting, she was up cleaning bottles, making formula, washing clothes, and trying to shower. Sleep was the last thing on her mind—until she ended up in the hospital from exhaustion. After two days in the hospital, she was sent back home, only for Malik to return with news that his job was facing budget cuts.

Yep, you heard it—Malik lost his job and couldn't afford to pay the rent. As they packed up their home and newborn, they were forced to move in with his aunt. Let's be clear—Malik's aunt already had a big family of her own, which meant all three of them had to squeeze into one room.

After about four job interviews, Malik finally landed a job. Before he even got his first paycheck, tax season rolled around. Once their refund hit, Malik took the whole amount and bought his family a two-bedroom townhome. While Tiffany was happy to finally be moving, she also wished he had taken her to see the place first. Things were going somewhat okay—baby Jaxon got his own room and started learning to walk. And yep, you guessed it—he lost that job too. And you can probably guess what happened next. Damn right—they had to move again, but this time, with his mother. Tiffany couldn't take it anymore. It's one thing to pack up and move, but doing it with a newborn? That was just way too much.

By now, baby Jaxon was about four years old, and things just kept getting worse. It seemed like every time they got their own place, Tiffany couldn't even decorate because she knew they would have to move again. So, Tiffany drove to the library, printed off divorce papers, filled them out, and paid $200 to get the ball rolling.

After being separated for a year, they finally went to court to finalize their divorce. Tiffany and Jaxon found their own two-bedroom apartment, and no matter how hard she worked, she refused to let anyone put her out again. Not only that, but she also created a new vision board and made a vow—*never*, and she meant *never*, would she move in with another man. It was time to focus on herself and her son, and if another man came into her life, she would be watching for all the red flags.

One day, while out with Jaxon, she saw Malik with another woman. All she could do was shake her head and say, *"Poor thing. If she only knew what she was getting herself into."* But guess what? Who cares! While he's out looking for the next woman he can use, she's out saying, *"Boy, bye"* to these no-good men.

2

Chapter

Jeremiah

"**Met her in the club, popping bottles, showing love.**" That was the song that would forever live in Tiffany's head. After everything she had been through, she decided it was time to love herself more and focus solely on Tiffany and her son—no men, no dating, no giving out her number, and nothing that involved a man. But the thing about being a rebound chick? They come when you're not looking.

Most people say that when you're not looking, that's when you find Mr. Right. In this case, he was damn sure Mr. Wrong. Meeting Jeremiah was never on her agenda. A few days before New Year's, Tiffany just wanted a night out alone for some "me time". While sitting at the bar, listening to music, and having a drink, she met Jeremiah—a short but cute guy with a low haircut and decent style. They wasted no time talking and exchanging numbers. Like all the others, he asked if he could take her on a date, and she agreed.

At this point, men were like grasshoppers—they come, they eat, and they leave. So, she knew exactly how she was going to treat him. Jeremiah came off as sweet and caring. He always asked if she needed anything and was right there to give it to her. After knowing each other for a short time, Tiffany invited Jeremiah over. She made sure she had a babysitter first because she wasn't ready for a man to be around her

Jeremiah

son. They didn't even realize it was New Year's when he came over for the first time.

After watching movies and chilling, it got late, and she agreed to let him spend the night. But she warned him: He better not try anything, or he was getting put out. While she was in the shower, she suddenly heard music playing and smelled her favorite candle. "I know this fool didn't just light my candle!" When Tiffany got out, she saw that Jeremiah had tried to set the mood for a good night—even though she had already told him not to try anything. The fact that Jeremiah had no idea how the night would play out didn't matter—he just wanted it to be special.

When Tiffany saw everything he had done for her, she knew exactly what to do. She went to her dresser, grabbed the biggest pair of grandma panties, a moo-moo nightgown, and put a bonnet on her head. Jeremiah just looked at her and laughed. "All that wasn't even called for," he said. "As long as we're both on the same page," she replied.

The next morning, Tiffany smelled food and said, "I know this man ain't cooking in my kitchen." When she walked in, she saw that he had made eggs, grits, and pancakes. As sweet as the gesture was, deep down, she wasn't really feeling it—but she sat down and ate anyway. During breakfast, Jeremiah asked how she slept. She shrugged. "It was okay, but you snore." *He* laughed. "Sorry, it's just that your bed is so soft and comfortable."

After breakfast, they cleaned the kitchen, Jeremiah left, and Tiffany went to the bathroom to get ready for the day. While at work, Tiffany got a text from Jeremiah asking if she wanted to come to his place that night for another night like yesterday. Since she didn't have to pick up her son until the weekend, she said yes. Tiffany wasn't really feeling the fact that she was packing an overnight bag, but she had already told herself that if she wasn't feeling it, she would leave—no questions asked. As she packed, she carefully chose everything she would take with her: an old pair of pajamas, a t-shirt and sweatpants, a toothbrush and toothpaste, washcloths and a towel, and her slippers.

When Jeremiah sent her the address, she looked up the area and saw that it wasn't the best. Not wanting to seem judgmental, she got in her car and headed to his place. When she arrived, she was already mad that she had to park on the side of the road. Good thing she had that old-school crowbar her grandfather had bought her.

As she walked up the steps and rang the doorbell, Tiffany was not prepared for what this man's house was going to look like. Yep, you guessed it—a hot-ass hood mess. Not only did this man live with his two brothers, but he didn't even have a bedroom. This grown-ass man slept in the living room on the couch, turning a sectional into a bed every night.

Tiffany asked if she could use the bathroom. Once inside, she immediately called Rachel and said, "I know you fucking lying." "Girl, why the hell does this man live with his brothers and sleep in the living room on the couch?" Rachel laughed. "Girl, go home, and whatever you do, don't give him none."

Trust and believe—that was the last thing on her mind. Tiffany hadn't had sex since Malik, and a man who slept on the couch was not about to change that. Jeremiah had popped some popcorn and started the movie. He had also turned the sectional into a bed, making it up with sheets and everything. Tiffany told herself she was going to make the best of it since he had put in the effort to make the night special.

As they watched the movie, one of Jeremiah's brothers walked into the kitchen and started fixing something to eat. Tiffany just looked over and said, "Seriously? Is he for real right now?" Jeremiah's brother caught the look on Tiffany's face and said, "Oh, my bad." Tiffany muttered under her breath, "This is some ghetto shit."

Well, at least she thought she had whispered it—because Jeremiah heard her. "Really?" he said. Tiffany couldn't say much except, "If you want me to leave, I will." Jeremiah shook his head. "Nah, you good. But that comment wasn't cool." After the movie, Tiffany told him she wanted to go home and that she'd talk to him tomorrow. When she got home, she ran and jumped into her bed. *As Tiffany drifted off to sleep, she thought, "Ain't no way that man thought I was going to sleep on a sectional and use a bathroom that two other men were sharing."*

The next day, Tiffany felt that it was best to slow things down with Jeremiah and only see him on her time. A few days had passed, and she didn't hear from him. She figured he just didn't want to have anything to do with her because of how she acted at his house. That is

Jeremiah

until he inboxed her on Facebook, saying his phone was off and he had to use his Wi-Fi to write her. Wow, really? Now, he knows he is too old not to pay his phone bill. He also wanted to see her and felt it was best to come to her place since clearly, she wasn't feeling his place at all. She responded back and told him he could come over, but he couldn't spend the night. When Jeremiah arrived at Tiffany's house, they both asked how their day was. "The last few days have been rough without a phone," Jeremiah sighed. "I bet," Tiffany said. When are you going to get your phone back on? "When I get paid," he responded.

Now, let's get one thing straight—Tiffany and Jeremiah had only been seeing each other for about three months with no title. So, they were both free to see and do whatever they wanted when they weren't around each other. However, on this particular day, things were going to change for these two.

Jeremiah began to express how these last three months had made him very happy and that she was the only person he enjoyed spending time with. He said he didn't want to go another day without making Tiffany his girlfriend.

Tiffany said to herself, "I have heard this bull crap before." She looked at him and said, "Let me guess, you also feel it's best that we move in together, too?" Jeremiah was not sure why she would think that, but she was feeling lonely, very vulnerable, and weak. She looked at him, and instead of saying yes, she said, "I thought I already was yours." Jeremiah picked Tiffany up, swung her around, and kissed her.

After her divorce, Tiffany had been single for 2 years. This time, she kept this relationship away from her friends because she didn't want to be questioned by them. She knew that she wasn't ready for a relationship. Jeremiah had none of the qualities on her list. This was getting ready to be a red flag and a hot mess of a relationship; all day long. When people say you'd better be following the signs, you'd better do just that. After only a few weeks of being a couple, Tiffany had not only been buying him lunch, but when she cooked dinner, she would make sure he had a plate. Every time she pulled up to his job, Jeremiah's coworkers would be standing outside every other day saying, "He got a good one."

One day, Jeremiah called Tiffany while she was at work and asked her if she could do something important for him. She had no idea what to expect when he said it was important. He had told her that his screen had cracked on his phone and that he needed to get a new phone. She said, "And you are telling me this because?" Jeremiah said he didn't have the extra money right now to buy a new phone because he and his brothers were looking for a bigger place, and he needed his extra money to go toward his place. So, why couldn't he just go to Walmart and get a cheap phone to hold him over? Who knows. Tiffany thought about it and told him she would get back to him. After work, she found herself in the parking lot of T-Mobile buying a grown-ass man a cell phone. When she called him and told him that she got the phone, he told her he would be by her house to get it when he got off.

She explained to him that the bill was $150 a month and due on the 15th of each month. Jeremiah said, "OK, that is fine." All that night, he kept telling her "Thank you". Now ask yourself this, "Do you really think he paid that phone bill?" This man had taken an old SIM card, put it in the new phone, and went back to paying fifty dollars a month. Yes, you heard it: fifty. Not only did she buy him a new phone she was stuck with the phone bill. But even with the food and the phone, that still was not enough to make Tiffany want to leave him.

Later that same month, Jeremiah and his brothers had gotten a bigger apartment, and he now had his own room. Tiffany couldn't wait to see her man's new place and, most importantly, his bedroom. So instead of packing her overnight bag with grandma pajamas, she thought she would change it up a bit and pull out her peek-a-boo lingerie. When she got to her man's apartment and went into his bedroom, she didn't care about the phone; she was ready to be all over her man. When she lay down on his bed, she noticed it was hard and was thinking maybe he just picked out a firm mattress. Please, tell me why this man only had a box spring and made it up with bed sheets like it was a mattress! Like she said, a red flag relationship.

By now, Tiffany was beyond blindsided by everything that she was dealing with. It really had gotten to the point that if he asked, she would do it. For a while, Tiffany had forgotten who she was and felt like a doormat. One day, Jeremiah was driving, and out of nowhere, his car started smoking. When he pulled over, he realized that his motor had blown and his car was going to be a total loss. While on the phone with the tow company, he texted Tiffany asking her to meet him so she could take him home. When she arrived, she asked him what had happened. Jeremiah already knew his car was a piece of crap, and it was just a matter of time before something happened. And you already know what his next request was. Before they even got to the house, Jeremiah was already begging and pleading that Tiffany get him a car.

Tiffany was at a loss for words because it was one thing to buy a phone… but a car?! This was a new level of disrespect. How does a grown man ask a woman to buy him a car? Jeremiah thought having sex and taking Tiffany out on a date was going to make her give in. Little did he know, he didn't even have to do all that because she was so blinded by "love" she didn't care. She was beyond mesmerized. Some may say she was under a spell. The next day, Tiffany went to pick Jeremiah up so they could go car shopping.

For the most part, he wasn't that picky when it came to knowing what he wanted. The first stop was looking at the Camaros. Unfortunately, he didn't see the color he wanted, so it was off to Dodge. What man wouldn't want a big Dodge Ram truck? Jeremiah saw the car he wanted from the stop sign. There it was, a 2022 black Dodge Ram truck with his name on it.

Tiffany couldn't put the car in park fast enough before he jumped out of the car like a kid in a candy store. When the salesman greeted them, Jeremiah was smiling from ear to ear, saying, "I already know what I want". The salesman walked them to the parking lot where the trucks were and told him the car he wanted was on sale for 22K. All he needed was $1,300 down. Jeremiah looked at the salesman and said, "My baby will be taking care of everything." When they went into the office, Tiffany had a gut feeling that this was not cool. When it was time to get her paperwork together, she heard a voice saying "You a crazy bitch if you do that." Just when she was getting ready to give the salesman her social, she looked at Jeremiah and said, "I can't do this." He looked at her and said, "Baby please don't do this." She told him buying a car is a big commitment and she didn't think they were at the place in their relationship where they should be making such big commitments.

Jeremiah insisted on them trying to have more options, just in case it was a money thing. Tiffany started to cry and said, " I just can't do it." Looking at him with tears in her eyes, she also wanted to know if he was even going to pay the car note. Especially since he dodged paying his phone bill. Jeremiah said, "Yes, I'm sure I will pay the car note; just trust me." She advised the car salesman that they would come back tomorrow and try everything again. When Tiffany dropped Jeremiah off, she went home and looked over at her vision board. Nowhere on this board did it say to find a man and pay his bills and buy him phones and cars.

Later that night, Jeremiah got a phone call from an ex. He didn't want to answer the phone but she sent him a text saying pick up the phone. When he finally called her back, she told him straight up, "I'm 7 weeks pregnant and it's yours." Jeremiah was numb and at a loss for words. How was he going to explain this to Tiffany? Now, instead of buying him a car, she is going to have to buy diapers. Jeremiah called an Uber and went straight to Tiffany's house, unannounced, to tell her the bad news. When he got to the house and rang the doorbell, he had no idea how this night was going to go. "What are you doing at my house?" "Can I come in? I need to talk to you," he begged. She let him in and led him to the kitchen, where she poured herself a glass of wine. After stalling, he finally began telling her about his ex-calling him. Slowly, he took her by the hand and said, "My ex is seven weeks pregnant, and I am the father."

Tiffany looked at him, laughed, and said, "You're joking, right?" Jeremiah said, "No, I wish I was. Still laughing, Jeremiah interrupted and asked, "What's so funny? She said, "You are." "You have been playing me and setting me up this whole time. First, it was the phone, then it was the lunches, then the car, and now you're having a baby! This is the game you tryna to play?" Tiffany started clapping and yelled out, "Get your shit and get the fuck out of my house!" Jeremiah was trying his hardest to get her to talk to him, but she was not having it. She just wanted him out of her life and far away from her. Jeremiah called Tiffany's phone over twenty times. She finally texted him and said, "Boy bye", and blocked him.

Even though she felt that she wanted to get back at him for everything she did, Tiffany wished Jeremiah nothing but the best of luck with his life. First, she had made sure she kept track of him using a fake Facebook page. Once she saw where his hangout spots were, she was ready to put her plan in motion. One night, she saw where he was going to be hanging out and sent her best friend there to meet him.

When her best friend Rachel arrived and saw Jeremiah, she went right up to him and started talking to him. When you're dealing with a broke nigga, they will fall for anything you tell them. She knew this was going to be easy as 1-2-3. Rachel and Jeremiah exchanged phone numbers and started talking. Easy bait is what she liked to call it. By this time, Jeremiah still had his phone, no car, and a brand-new baby. Rachel knew how to work her magic. During their first phone conversation, she had told him he looked familiar and looked him up and saw that he knew Tiffany. When she mentions Tiffany's name to him, he wasn't sure what to expect. Little did he know, in order to date Rachel, he was going to have to put in some work, and she wasn't talking about sex.

After a few dates and hanging out, Rachel got all of Tiffany's money back. If he was going to play the game, she was going to play the game too, boo. The fact that he really thought Rachel was into him was one thing, but for him to pay the money back, thinking he was going to get a great woman out of it in return? "Boy bye! Ain't going to happen...Who's next?"

3

Chapter

At this point, you would have thought Tiffany had had enough when it came to dating, but in this case, the search was not over. A typical day at the bank changed for the better. While standing in line, Tiffany looked over and saw a tall, bald-headed guy standing at the teller. Normally, she would wait for them to approach her, but this time, she decided to change the game and ask him for his number. Without hesitation, she walked up to him and said, "Hey, how are you? I know you're busy and have to go, but would you mind if we exchange numbers?" Without wasting any time, he gave her his number and told her his name was Elijah.

While talking on the phone, Elijah explained to Tiffany that he was going through a divorce and was currently living with his aunt. She told him she had been there and done that. She shared that she had been married for five years and had a son. He explained that he had been married for seven years and had four children. Talking to someone who had something in common with her made her feel better.

After a few late-night conversations on the phone, Elijah asked Tiffany if she wanted to get some drinks. On the night they were supposed to go out, Tiffany was trying to figure out what to do with her hair and what to wear. She decided on a two-strand twist and put on some jeans and a shirt. When Elijah texted Tiffany to see if 8 p.m.

would be fine to meet up, she got a call from Jeremiah. When she answered, he asked if he could help her with something. She had completely forgotten that she had unblocked him when she got her money back from him. She quickly made sure to put his number back on the block list and focused on what Elijah was bringing to the table.

Around 7 p.m., Tiffany started getting ready to go have drinks with Elijah. She didn't even know where they were going yet. As time went by, she realized it was almost 8 p.m., and she still hadn't heard from him. After two hours, Elijah finally reached out, apologizing and asking if they could meet up at Applebee's to grab something to eat really quickly. At first, Tiffany didn't want to go because she felt that Applebee's was not where you go for a date. Since she just wanted drinks, she agreed. When she arrived, Elijah got out of the car wearing basketball shorts, a T-shirt, and thong flip-flops. Tiffany immediately wanted to get back in her car! She thought to herself, "This was not how he was dressed at the bank. How can someone go from wearing a three-piece suit to looking like they're getting ready to eat and then go straight to bed afterward?"

Elijah walked over to Tiffany, gave her a hug, and apologized for the late hour. "I'm sorry for asking you out so late. I had a late Zoom call that I had to attend, and it went longer than expected." Tiffany smiled but silently thought to herself, "That's fine and all, but he could have at least put on some jeans." However, she decided to make the best of it and enjoy the drinks, even though they'd probably taste watered down.

After about three drinks and some appetizers, Tiffany was ready to call it a night and head home. Elijah could tell she felt some type of way about the way he was dressed. While walking her to her car, he asked to take her on a real date and promised he wouldn't be wearing basketball shorts to the next one. Once again, this was the guy she felt she wanted to keep to herself. As much as she loved telling her friends about the newest chapter in her life, some things she liked to keep private.

Elijah had asked Tiffany if she liked pasta, and while huffing and puffing, she said, "Yes, I do." Tiffany said to herself, "I know this man is not about to take me to no damn Olive Garden. I guess it's true what they say—just because they're at the bank doesn't mean they have money." And Elijah was definitely coming off with broke vibes.

Little did she know, she was so wrong. Elijah was not broke at all. What Tiffany thought was going to be pasta from Olive Garden was actually dinner from a high-end, expensive restaurant called LA Pierre. Oh, and let's not forget—the man showed up in a nice suit with flowers. After enjoying their amazing meal, Tiffany asked Elijah if he would like to come back to her place.

At this point, Tiffany was in a phase where she was just saying what she wanted and not worrying about the outcome. As long as he didn't ask her to buy anything or pay a bill, she was good. Too bad Elijah wasn't on the same page. He smiled and told her he was going to call it a night, ending things with a hug and a kiss on the cheek. Tiffany mumbled to herself, "Oh, so he's playing hard to get now?". But honestly? She kind of liked that he was respectful—even though nothing was going to happen anyway. A few days passed, and Elijah hit her up, asking if she wanted to come to his sister's house for a game night. "Yeah, I'll come. Send me the address," she replied.

Before heading over, Tiffany called him. "You need me to bring anything?" "Nah, we got everything," Elijah assured her. When she pulled up, she was just ready to have a good time. Three hours of back-to-back games, food, and drinks later, she was tapped out. It was time to go—her sister was back at her house watching Jaxson, and she wasn't trying to be out all night.

As Tiffany was getting ready to say goodbye, someone handed her a chocolate ball with an interesting taste. It wasn't bad, but she could tell it was something she'd never had before. She ended up eating two of them, and before she knew it, she had passed out on the couch. Later, she found out that she had been high—they were weed balls. Elijah had carried Tiffany into the bedroom to sleep it off. Little did she know, that night would also be their first time together. And no, she wasn't forced into anything—she knew exactly what she was doing. When she woke up, she had ten missed calls and a bunch of text messages from her sister. As soon as she got in the car, she called her sister and told her about the crazy night she had.

Tiffany couldn't wait to take a shower and wash away the events of the night. But as the warm water ran over her, her mind kept drifting back to Elijah—how amazing he was. She could still feel his lips kissing her from head to toe and the way he took his time with her body. For the first time in a long time, she felt special. Before she

Elijah

knew it, just thinking about him had caused her to climax in the shower.

Later that day, Elijah called to check on her. "I had no idea there was going to be weed at the party," he told her. "My sister had a friend visiting from out of town, and she wanted everyone to try them." "Oh, okay," Tiffany laughed. "I'll come to the movie parties, but they can leave the weed at home." They both laughed it off and started talking about when they would see each other again.

Elijah invited Tiffany to the flea market because he had a few things he wanted to pick up. She agreed to meet him there, but this time, Elijah insisted on picking her up from her house. Hesitant at first, she finally agreed and sent him her address. At least this time, Jaxon was visiting his grandparents. When Elijah pulled up in an all-black Escalade truck, Tiffany looked at the massive vehicle and thought to herself, 'I'm going to need a step stool."

As they got in the truck, the music started playing, setting the mood. Tiffany, though, had something on her mind. After three months of talking, she still wasn't sure where this was going. "So, what are we doing?" she asked, cutting straight to the point. Elijah didn't even hesitate. "I'm just trying to have fun since I'm still going through a divorce." "Oh, so that's what this is?" The only thing running through Tiffany's mind now was the possibility of him going back to his wife. Divorce ain't even final yet; that's a recipe for disaster.... At this point, you would've thought she was turning into Joan from Girlfriends—overthinking everything instead of just living in the moment.

After realizing that things had to flow naturally, Tiffany decided it was best to just take things one day at a time. The last thing she wanted was to get hurt again and feel like she had wasted her time. The more time she spent with Elijah, the more she felt like she had nothing to worry about. Everything was good—until one day, out of nowhere, the calls just stopped. No warning. No explanation. Just silence. Every time she called, it went straight to voicemail. No response to texts.

"Damn, I knew I shouldn't have given it up to him. And in the back seat of a car, at that," she muttered to herself, feeling beyond ashamed. Tiffany, you are not in high school, and your knees do not work like that no more," she said to herself.

Three weeks passed, and just when she was about to let it go, her phone rang from an unknown number. She hesitated, then answered. "Hey, sweetie, I got a new number," Elijah's voice came through like nothing had happened. She didn't know how to feel. Part of her wanted to curse him out. The other part? Well… the other part was feeling lonely. As much as she wanted to ask where he had been, she just swept it under the rug and saw him when he asked. Tiffany knew she was a beautiful woman. She wasn't in love or anything—she just missed the company and conversation.

Regrettably, just like before, the calls stopped again. And then, yet again, he popped back up with another new number. Not once. Not twice. But three times. At this point, the only thing she kept asking herself was *"Why?" and "What is this man doing that he keeps changing his number?"* When she was finally ready to ask him why he kept changing his number, he hit her with the most ridiculous excuse. "Oh, I just keep getting too many scam calls." She stared at her phone, blinking; no words.

At this point, she knew it was time to leave him right where he was because nothing about this man was changing. Unless he thought she had *"Boo Boo the Fool"* written across her forehead, it was officially time to say—"Boy, bye."

4

Chapter

Caleb

One, two, three, and now four. Tiffany was officially at her breaking point with men. That was until Caleb came into her life. She walked past him at work every day and never paid him any attention. But one day, she thought, *What's the worst that can happen?* A few drinks and dinner with a coworker wouldn't hurt.

The first time they went out, the conversation was light—just work talk, complaining about their never-ending quarter projects. Little did Tiffany know, Caleb had been waiting years for this moment. He had always noticed the pain in her eyes when she came to work, but he never brought it up. Instead, he made it a point to tell her she looked nice every day and hoped she had a good one. On rough days, he'd even have a rose sent to her office. She thought he was a little rough around the edges, but he wasn't bad-looking. *Ain't nothing wrong with having a tall, dark chocolate man on your arm.*

One day, while sitting in a board meeting, Tiffany listened as her boss talked about cutbacks and layoffs. She had been with the company for eight years, worked hard for every promotion, and was finally in line for the next step up. After the meeting, she headed back to her office, only to see Caleb walking in—with boxes in his hands. "They let me go," he said, shaking his head. "Budget cuts." Tiffany was stunned.

Caleb

She and Caleb had been secretly dating for six months, and she was finally getting used to being in a committed relationship again. This *was not* about to be another *Malik situation*. But she really liked Caleb. And for once, she wanted to prove to a man that she had his back. The next day, she logged into her laptop and maxed out her dependents—even though she only had one child. Then, she made a trip to Dollar Tree, grabbed a calendar and a notebook, and wrote down all of his bills. After that, she started making sacrifices—cutting down on personal spending—to make sure her man was good while he looked for work.

At first, Caleb was on it. Up at 8 AM every morning, applying for jobs, fixing up his resume. But as time passed… things changed. A whole year went by. Caleb was still unemployed. Eventually, 8 AM turned into 12 PM, and looking for jobs turned into just checking emails. And then, one day, he came to Tiffany with a business idea. He wanted to start his own trucking company and needed about $3,000 to get started. The crazy part about this whole plan? Caleb had no education or training in running a business. *So yep, this was about to be an epic failure.* They spent countless days going over his plan, but Tiffany knew it was a load of crap. In just one year, their relationship had done a full 360. At this point, she might as well make an appointment at the tattoo parlor and get **ATM** inked across her forehead—because that's exactly what she had become.

Just when you thought things couldn't get worse… they did. While on her way to Caleb's house, Tiffany's phone rang. "Babe, a tow truck is here trying to take my car," Caleb said, panic in his voice. *Tiffany was confused.* How was his car getting repossessed when she had been the one paying the note? Not knowing what else to do, she told him to hold tight until she got there. But by the time she pulled into the driveway, it was too late. The tow truck was already driving away— with Caleb's car hooked to the back.

That was the first time Tiffany had ever seen a man cry over losing something. Tears streamed down Caleb's face as he beat himself up over it. "Don't worry. We'll get through this," Tiffany reassured him. The next day, Caleb was already looking at cars he wanted—as if he even had a plan to pay for one, let alone show proof of income. Yep, you guessed it. This was Elijah all over again.

By now, Tiffany and Caleb had been together for two years, and she was still taking care of him. At first, she thought about getting a loan from the bank to help him out, but she messed that up by telling them she wasn't going to be the driver. Then they checked Craigslist, but every car had too many miles or was too far away. Finally, they came across a buy-here, pay-here dealership. At first, Caleb didn't like anything on the lot, but he knew he needed a car. After circling the same cars over and over, he finally said, "I'm ready to go. I don't like nothing here." Tiffany couldn't understand it. How is a man with nothing going to be this picky? After dropping Caleb back home, Tiffany drove straight back to that same dealership, picked out a Chrysler 300, and put down $1,200. As she signed the paperwork, she might as well have had DUMB tattooed on her forehead. Since she couldn't drive two cars at once, she called a friend to come pick her up.

The next day, Tiffany pulled up to Caleb's house and yelled out, "Surprise!" Caleb stepped outside, staring at the car. "Bae, whose car is this?" "I said, "Surprise!" Clearly, Caleb was not happy. "That's not the car I wanted," he said, shaking his head. "Take it back." But she couldn't. The dealership had a five-day trade policy, but no returns. That morning, Caleb drove Tiffany home and told her, "I'll just call for a ride if I need to go somewhere." Tiffany knew there was nothing wrong with that car. It just wasn't what he wanted.

Two weeks passed before Caleb finally came to his senses. "I changed my mind," he told her. "I'll take the car." Oh, now he wanted it? She was beyond pissed that it took him two whole weeks to realize he needed transportation. And let's not forget—not only did she put the down payment down, but she was also the one responsible for the car note. Yeah, you heard it right. Another $320 was added to her already long list of bills.

Caleb knew he had to make it up to her. So, he cooked her a nice meal and gave her a massage. And while that was nice and all, Tiffany was still pissed. Four months passed. She had paid every single car note, plus car insurance. And this man still had no job. All Caleb wanted to do was get his truck business off the ground. And just like that, three years of dating had passed. Tiffany was down to her last $2,000.

In those three years, she had taken out loans, pulled from her 401(k), changed her dependents, paid every single bill, bought him a car, and even gave him money for his business. And for what? To go nowhere. At this point, there weren't enough home-cooked meals, back rubs, 'I love you's, or late-night sex in the world to make up for this. Tiffany had officially hit rock bottom. She could've just stayed married to Malik if she was gonna put up with this. This was not a relationship. This was not a partnership. This was what being used looked like. Every night before bed, Tiffany would look in the mirror and say, "Damn. How much more can a bitch take?" And the answer? A whole notha' year.

After being together for four years, Tiffany finally decided to end things with Caleb. She even took back the car and had it repossessed. She'd rather mess up her credit than keep paying on a car he wasn't even appreciative of. And guess what? He never started his trucking business either. So, four months after ending the relationship, Tiffany found out that this man got a job at a call center. A fucking call center. Over $20,000 she put into their relationship, and this man is working in customer service, answering phones. Boy, bye.

5

Chapter

Aaron

As you can see, Tiffany just couldn't win when it came to dating or relationships. At this point, the vision boards weren't working, getting advice from her friends wasn't working, nor watching inspirational videos. Everything she ever wanted in a man just seemed to not exist. There was nowhere else to turn to, and she had given up.

One day, she took a leap of faith, got dressed, and went to church. Who knows when the last time Tiffany had stepped foot inside a church was? If it wasn't a funeral or wedding, Sunday mornings were reserved for the bed. She had never attended this church before, but the praise and worship team were pretty good, and the sermon was somewhat decent. One thing is for sure—no woman likes going to church thinking the Pastor is going to know exactly what she's going through. So, what she thought was going to be a sermon about being single turned out to be a sermon for the married people.

After church was dismissed, Tiffany found herself in the drive-thru of Silver Bay and then grabbed a bottle of wine. When she got home and changed into her cozy clothes, she sat down to watch TV. While watching her favorite movie, *Two Can Play That Game*, she began scrolling on TikTok. She saw so many dating apps that were tempting her to try. Online dating was never in her cards—she thought it was scary and creepy. But just like that, Christian Mingle popped up on her newsfeed. The first thing she thought was, "Who's spending $8 a week to meet people?" At this point, it was the only thing left she hadn't tried. She downloaded the free trial and created a profile. She kept it cute and simple—one to three pictures and limited information on her bio.

After about three days of scrolling, she had a few matches—one white, one black, and one Hispanic. Now, even though all of them were nice-looking guys, none of them were what she was looking for. However, Tiffany knew that if she wanted things to work out with Christian Mingle, she had to hurry up. A 7-day trial can go by really quickly when you're not actively looking. And just like that, on day 7, she found a match. There he was—Aaron, 35, light skin, low haircut, medium height, and a Black man. And just like before, she reached out first by saying hi. She didn't have time for small talk in the chat room, so she gave him her number and waited for him to call. Trying to keep herself busy so that she wouldn't have her phone in her hand all day waiting, after a whole week, he finally sent her a text saying, "Hello, how are you? My name is Aaron."

They would talk on the phone for hours, laughing and telling jokes to each other. Ain't no way she was having this much fun on the phone with a man she had never met before. She found herself laughing harder than she had with men she'd met in public. They decided to have their first date downtown and sit by the waterfalls. He brought a blanket because it was cold outside. That right there made her feel special—just by those small things. Talking about their likes and dislikes, and where they saw themselves in the next five years. These were conversations she had never had before with anyone. Could this be the man on her vision board that she had been overlooking?

One day, Aaron asked Tiffany how she felt about Dru Hill. She told him she loved them and already knew they were on tour with Jodeci. Aaron was glad she said she liked them because he had already bought the tickets for the concert. "Damn, he's trying to have long-term goals," she said. The concert was four months out, and they had only known each other for three short weeks. Hey, it was his money, so she wasn't going to judge. And if things didn't work out between them, it's not like he couldn't find someone else to go with.

Unfortunately, he didn't have to take anyone else because they made it to four months. At the concert, Tiffany sang every song and tried to do every hop and jump she could. Aaron was loving the look and smile on her face. Not only did he feel this was real, but he had a vision board at home himself. And for the first time, this was a man who was not in any rush to invite her over to his place, and she didn't invite him to hers either. After the show, Tiffany was in the mood for some late-night tacos. And no, they didn't come from Taco Bell. The joy of living in Texas is you can always find a late-night food truck somewhere.

While eating their tacos, Aaron looked at Tiffany and told her these five months of getting to know her had been amazing, and wanted to know if she would do him the honor of being his girlfriend. She looked into his eyes and said yes, jumping up to hug him. After all the men she had doubted over the last three years, she was finally about to call her friends and tell them she had a man.

That same night, Tiffany invited Aaron over to her place for a nightcap. Soft music and wine were how the night was supposed to go. But even though he never asked, Tiffany's hormones were shooting to the moon. While lying in bed, reflecting on how good the night had gone, Tiffany's mind was somewhere else. And baby, after some kissing and a little foreplay, this man whipped it out proudly, and all she saw was a Roku remote in between his legs. Oh, hell no. But Tiffany needed this, so she was going to take what she could get and call it a day. And it wasn't much. And it kept falling out, so yep, that meant no sex in this relationship. Aaron thought he was Superman in them sheets, but he was really Michael from *Waiting to Exhale*. How in the world was Tiffany going to tell Aaron that he was an amazing man, but she didn't want sex in their relationship? This was going to be a rough one. Maybe they'd just have so much fun hanging out together that he wouldn't think about it.

Tiffany was coming up with every excuse in the book not to sleep with Aaron. From her period being on, to saying she had a yeast infection, saying she was tired, or just the classic "No." She knew she wasn't going to be able to keep these lies going, so she finally decided to tell him how he'd feel if they didn't have sex in their relationship. Aaron was surprised and didn't understand where this was coming from. Tiffany explained that she wanted to grow and build their relationship spiritually, and that meant no sex. For the most part, Aaron agreed, but deep down, he wasn't feeling that at all. It eventually got to the point where he couldn't handle it and told Tiffany that if they couldn't have sex, then they couldn't be together. Tiffany was crushed and hurt. How do you tell a man who's so nice and respectful that his penis is small? She didn't want to let him go, but she had no choice. She called Rachel and told her what happened. Rachel told her maybe one day he would find someone who liked his little Roku remote control.

After being apart for about three days, Tiffany started missing Aaron badly and decided to call him. She wanted to work things out with him, but Aaron was focused on his clothing business. His business had been doing exceptionally well, and during those last three days, he had been grinding hard. Tiffany's birthday was the following month, and she didn't want to spend it alone, so she reached out to Aaron to see if he wanted to spend it with her. He told her he'd get back to her and let her know if he wasn't busy. Around 8 PM, he texted her saying he would come by. Tiffany ran to her room and put on some cute fishnet stockings, and a matching bra and panty set.

When Aaron came to her house, he told her he couldn't stay long. Tiffany said that was fine, and they did their usual—soft music and wine. But this time, all she was getting from Aaron was soft music and wine. She had no idea why he wasn't turned on by what she was wearing. Not that he couldn't keep his eyes off her, he knew that he didn't want it. She tried pushing up on him, but he pushed her away.

Lost for words, Tiffany had no idea where all this was coming from. After about two hours and a few more glasses of wine, Aaron felt it was time to leave. All they did was talk about how much fun they had when they were together and how they missed each other. But nothing they talked about made Aaron want to touch her. Instead, he gave her a hug and kissed her on the forehead. She couldn't believe what had just happened and felt more embarrassed than anything. After having a horrible birthday, Tiffany decided to treat herself to a spa day. And you would never guess who she ran into. Yep, you guessed it—Aaron—and he wasn't alone. "Are you ready, baby?" There it was: another woman standing there with the man that used to be hers. Tiffany's mouth hit the floor, and she couldn't get out of that spa fast enough. "Have fun with your Roku remote control. Boy, bye!"

Chapter 6

Carter

Stop, look, and listen—this was the only thing Tiffany was doing at this point in her life. She was making sure to read the signs and calling her friends for advice. But most importantly, she wanted to get back into church. The only man she wanted in her life was God and nobody else. After being married and meeting man after man, Tiffany was starting to feel like a hoe, low-key. Even though some of the guys she dated were in committed relationships that just didn't work, she had hit rock bottom. The only thing that was going to get her back to a focused state of mind was prayer and cutting men off; completely. She needed to learn to date herself and find Tiffany again. Going to church and not only listening to the words but taking notes made her feel closer to God every day. Every Sunday, she would call her Grandma Jean and talk about how she really enjoyed the service. Of course, her grandma would ask her if she had found a nice man at church. Tiffany's answer would always be no.

One day, Tiffany got a call that her grandma had fallen and had to go to the ER. Tiffany's grandma was her rock and the glue to the family. When she got to the hospital, the doctor said her diabetes was acting up and she needed to take more insulin. Tiffany knew right then that she wanted to move her grandma in with her. Since she wasn't seeing anybody, it wasn't going to be a problem. Once she got her grandma settled in and hired someone to come watch her while she worked, Tiffany knew there was no room for dating. When getting off work, she would make sure to pick up dinner for her son and grandma. This had become her new norm. However, that didn't last too long. About six months later, Ms. Jean's diabetes took a turn for the worse, and that spring, she passed away. What was Tiffany to do with her family, feeling destroyed? Not only did she stop going to church, but she started losing focus on what she was supposed to be doing in life. Instead of taking herself out, she called her girls and partied until she passed out.

One day, while getting coffee out of the break room, her coworker, Carter, wanted to check on her to see how she was doing. "Good morning, Tiffany, how are you doing today?" he said. She replied that she was fine and walked away with a hard eye roll. Carter was someone she never looked at because she knew he was in a relationship. This pattern continued for a minute, to the point where Tiffany started buying her coffee before coming to work. While coming off the elevator one morning, Carter bumped into Tiffany and spilled coffee all over her blouse. Can you say pissed to the max? "You need to watch where you're going," Tiffany said. "My bad, I'll try to be careful next time," said Carter. Lucky for Tiffany, she had an extra shirt in her drawer. Of course, throughout the day, Carter kept saying he was sorry.

As the day came to an end, Carter asked if he could take Tiffany out to replace her coffee. Tiffany looked at him and said, "Sure, as long as your girlfriend is coming." Carter laughed and said he was single. "How long has it been?" she asked. "Not too long," he replied. "But don't worry, we're done, done," he said. So, Tiffany took him up on his offer. Sitting inside Starbucks, Tiffany wanted to know what happened between Carter and his ex. "She was always turning her phone over and turning the ringer off when we went out. Whenever I would ask about it, she said it was nothing. I thought she was cheating, so after five long years, I broke up with her."

"Damn, that's messed up," Tiffany said. "It's cool, we were already having problems anyway," Carter replied. "So now we just co-parent for our child," Carter added. Tiffany didn't really care too much about what he was talking about because she had enough on her plate. The only thing she was worrying about doing was planning her grandma Jean's balloon release for her birthday.

"So, Tiffany, tell me a little bit about yourself," Carter asked. She looked at him and said, "Like you don't already know. You know I used to date Caleb, and I'm not trying to be the job's pass-around girl." With a small laugh, Carter said, "Who's trying to pass you around? I'm just trying to get to know you." Tiffany began crying and started talking about her grandma. Carter picked up a napkin, wiped her face, and told her he had no idea. She told him it was okay. He said, "If you want, I'll chill with you after the balloon release." She told him she'd let him know when everything was over with.

On the day of her grandma's birthday, Tiffany thought it was best to take the day off and stay home. Carter texted her, saying everything was going to be okay and that he was still available if she wanted to chill. The fact that he even remembered put a smile on her face. After the balloon release, she called Carter before she made it to the car. She was going to ask him to meet her at the park, but it was getting cold, so she told him to meet her at Starbucks. With no hesitation, he agreed, and they pulled in at the same time.

Tiffany cried the whole way while driving to Starbucks. When Carter got out of the car, he came over to Tiffany, opened her door, and just held her as tight as he could. She asked if he would just sit in the car with her. As she kept crying and started talking about her grandma, Carter gently kissed her forehead. When he kissed her forehead, Tiffany leaned back as he said he was sorry and didn't mean to overstep. Tiffany slowly kissed him back. They kissed for a while, and when they stopped, Tiffany felt it was best to just go home alone. Carter told her goodnight and said he would see her tomorrow.

When Tiffany got home, she didn't know how to feel and hoped he didn't think something was happening between them. Tiffany wanted to at least stay committed to being off men. The next day at work, Tiffany received some flowers sent to her office with a card that said, "I'm always one call away. Love, Carter." She texted him and said, "Thank you."

After spending a little more time together, Tiffany started thinking that this man was kind of sweet and okay to hang with. One day, she invited him over to her place to chill and watch movies. He agreed to come over, and when he did, they talked, laughed, and watched movies, not even realizing how fast the time had gone by. Carter didn't leave her house until 5 a.m. Good thing it was the weekend because he would've been late for work. Now, one thing is for sure: this man had the juiciest lips ever. Kissing him felt like sex. Come on, ladies, you know what I mean. We've all been there before.

Unsurprisingly, things started changing between them, and not in a good way. He started having excuses for why he couldn't see her. Using his daughter, or saying stuff needed to be done at his house, or that he was catching up on work—there was always something. Lucky for Tiffany, she was already two steps ahead of him.

Tiffany went on social media and found Carter's ex. With hesitation, she reached out to her, asking if everything was okay with Carter. Her message said;

I know you don't know me, but me and Carter have been talking for about a month now, and I haven't heard from him. I just wanted to make sure he was okay.

The ex's response wasn't quite what she was looking for:

Why are you messaging me? And yes, he's fine. He's been staying at my house, and we're back together.

Tiffany had never been the type to go back and forth with another woman, especially on social media, so instead she called Carter, but got his voicemail. The bad part was that she had never been to his house, so that wasn't an option. She found out that he would be back to work that Monday, so she decided to wait. That felt like the longest weekend ever. When Monday came, Tiffany couldn't wait to see his light-skinned self walk past her office.

When she saw him, she told him to come into her office. As soon as Carter sat down, she said, "Your phone must be broke." He replied, "It fell in the water while cleaning the dishes." Tiffany looked at him and said, "Damn, that must've been hard, not being able to talk to your child." Before he could get another word out, she put him on blast and told him she already knew he got back with his ex. "It's not what you think," he said. He explained that his ex invited him over to talk and wanted to know if they could work things out. Carter told Tiffany he told his ex he would think about it. Tiffany shot back, "The bigger question is why would you tell her you'd think about it if you've been trying to have something with me?"

Carter looked at her and said he never meant to hurt her; he just got caught up in a love triangle. Tiffany just stared at him and told him to get out of her office. She told him that she wished them nothing but the best and hoped his ex wouldn't cheat this time.

Carter kept trying to tell Tiffany that they weren't fully back together, but Tiffany wasn't having it. "So, what you're not gonna do is string me along while you figure it out," she said. "Because, baby, I can do bad all by myself. Boy, bye!"

Chapter 7

boy bye

Tiffany Jackson, as you can see, has had her share of experiences with men—both good and bad. Sometimes, we as women have to understand that it's okay to be alone. No one will look at you differently if you're in a relationship or single. Sometimes, the single life is even better than a relationship. And while there are some relationships worth saving, my grandma once told me, "Don't let no man walk all over you and treat you like you're a stove on the back burning."

It's okay to take your time and get to know someone. Make that vision board and follow the goals and desires you want in a man. The right one will come, and trust me, you'll know it. Because that will be the one who won't let you go, no matter how tough things get. You just have to ask yourself: Do you want a God-fearing man, or do you want to keep being the rebound chick?

One love, stay up, and keep your eyes open.

www.ingramcontent.com/pod-product-compliance
Lightning Source LLC
LaVergne TN
LVHW010416070526
838199LV00064B/5316